The Fox in the Box

Written by Amanda Gee

Illustrations by Lee Holland

This book is dedicated to all those wonderful people who stand up and speak out for those without a voice.

The rain fell down in great big blobs
On the home of the fox in the cardboard box.

He was tired and lonely and felt very bad,
And when he thought of his family
he felt very sad.

BUMP!
ROAR!
THUD!

He had run away as fast as he could
When he'd heard the loud noises
in the dark, scary wood.

A little girl called Lydia heard a sobbing sound,

So she crept very slowly close to the ground,

Then, very gently, she opened the box ...

And out crept the frightened and confused little fox.

"Oh dear, little fox,
what's upset you so much?"
As she reached down to him
with a comforting touch.
She spoke softly and said
"Please, please don't you cry,
I am sure I can help
well, at least I can try!"

The fox said, "I'm lost and I'm scared. What can I do? My family will wonder where I am, too."

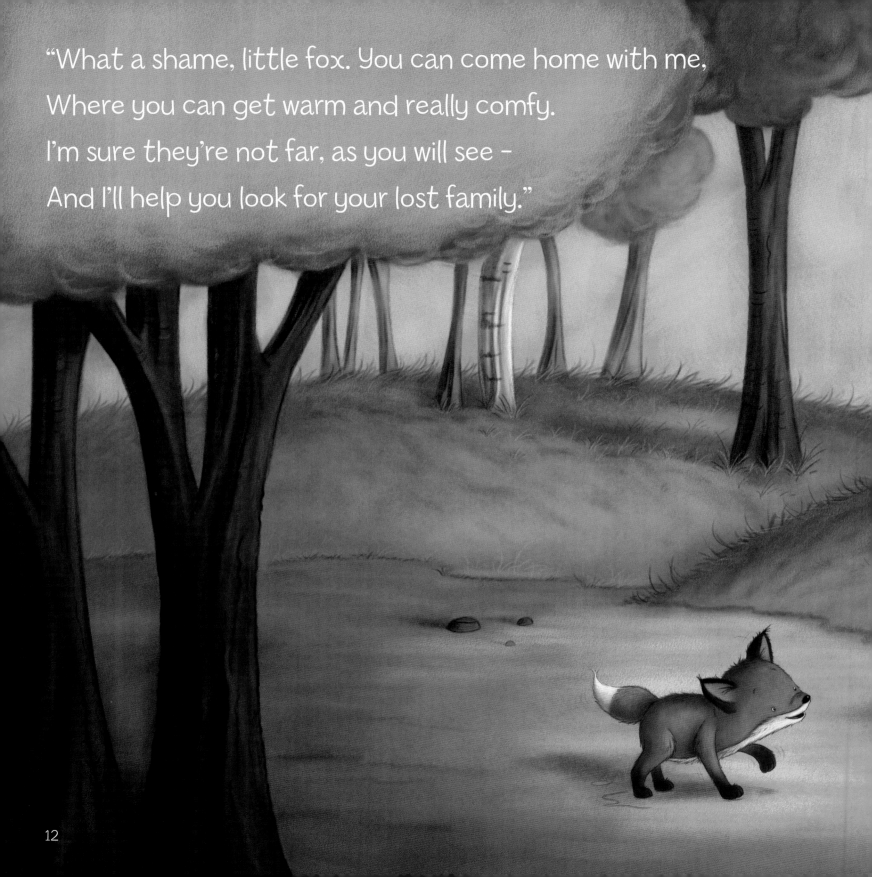

"What a shame, little fox. You can come home with me,
Where you can get warm and really comfy.
I'm sure they're not far, as you will see –
And I'll help you look for your lost family."

The fox looked up and smiled in delight.
"I think I would like that, yes, I think that I might!"
The little fox felt a warm fuzzy feeling –
This kind offer sounded very appealing.

13

The very next day they searched through the wood,
Gathering stories and tales – as much as they could.

They didn't find Mum,
but met badgers and moles
And lots of other creatures
who'd lost their cosy old holes.

The animals were worried and very annoyed
Because their green leafy wood was being destroyed.
So they all got together to decide what to do
About the diggers and men and the hullabaloo.

Lydia got busy telling all who would hear
Of her plans to save the foxes, the badgers and deer.

The people were sad and very angry, too,
When they heard of these plans
that came out of the blue.

"Oh, no!" they all said. "We're not happy with this.

Those beautiful woods will be very missed!

We'd all rather see the bugs and the bees

And the birds in the trees

Than concrete and roads that are bad news for toads."

20

Posters were made for everyone to see
And the whole village got involved in saving the trees.

Everyone shouted and sang, and banners were waved,
Until finally the wood and the wildlife were saved.

"WE DID IT!" they shouted. "HURRAY!" was the cry.

And they all wept buckets as they said their goodbyes.

Only the poor little fox was left feeling sad.

"I still haven't found my mum or my dad!"

A rustle was heard in the bushes ahead,
Then out of the darkness he saw his mum tread.

"Thank goodness we've found you!"
she cried in delight
As the rest of his family came into sight.

This wasn't the end for Lydia and the fox

Who no longer needed the cardboard box.

"Thank you," said the fox, "Friends always we will be ...

With me helping you and you helping me."

The little fox was happier than he ever thought he'd be,

as he drifted off to sleep

dreaming of Lydia and his much loved family.